RAGGEDY ANN
AND THE
HOBBY HORSE

WORTH GRUELLE

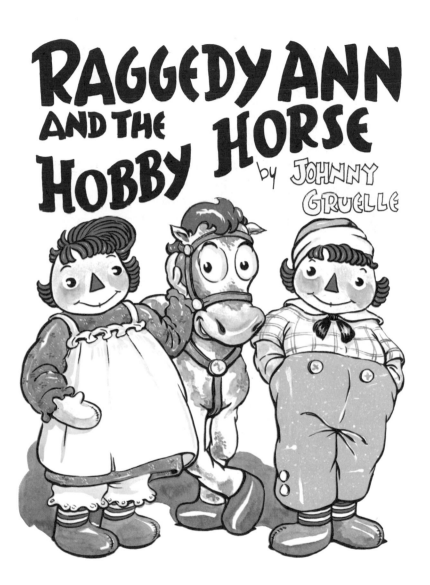

RAGGEDY ANN
AND THE
HOBBY HORSE

by JOHNNY GRUELLE

A YEARLING BOOK

YEARLING BOOKS are designed especially to entertain and enlighten young people. The finest available books for children have been selected under the direction of Charles F. Reasoner, Professor of Elementary Education, New York University.

For a complete listing of all Yearling titles, write to Education Sales Department, Dell Publishing Co., Inc., 1 Dag Hammarskjold Plaza, New York, N.Y. 10017.

Published by
Dell Publishing Co., Inc.
1 Dag Hammarskjold Plaza
New York, New York 10017

ISBN: 0-440-47327-6

Reprinted by arrangement with The Bobbs-Merrill Company, Inc.
Printed in the United States of America
Third Dell Printing—August 1978

CHAPTER 1

IT WAS A COOL, bright summer morning, and the sun was just sending its first sunbeams down to wake the flowers. Raggedy Ann and Raggedy Andy, resting under the shade of a giant maple tree, sat up suddenly.

Raggedy Ann poked Raggedy Andy. "Listen! What is that funny noise?"

Cloppity-clop, clumpity-clump came the sound along the path not far from the leafy green maple. *Clippity-clop, clippity-clop, cloppity-clip* came the sound again. Then it stopped. The Raggedys wondered who or what was making the queer noise. Then they heard a loud sob and a very sad sigh. *Cloppity-clop, clumpity-clump,* the sound echoed again. And now heavy footsteps were quite close to where they were sitting under the friendly old maple.

Raggedy Ann wondered, "Whoever can it be? It doesn't sound like any woodland creature we've met!"

Raggedy Ann suggested, "Perhaps it is an elephant."

"Oh no, Raggedy Ann, there are no elephants in the forest!" Raggedy Andy said.

"Chirp, chirp," called a redbird sitting on a bough overhead, "I can see a funny-looking four-legged creature hobbling up the path. He looks like a horse, but not quite like any horse I have ever seen. Here he comes now!"

And there, right before the Raggedys, stood a wooden Hobby Horse! Big tears were rolling down his cheeks and he did indeed look very unhappy.

Raggedy Ann and Raggedy Andy ran to the poor sad creature, wiped his tears with their pretty hankies, and then threw their arms around his neck. "There, there, don't cry so. We'll help you if you will tell us what the trouble is. But first tell us who you are and where you live."

Raggedy Ann tried to comfort the wooden Hobby Horse so that he would cheer up. Raggedy Andy and Raggedy Ann did not like to see anyone sad or unhappy. They were always so cheerful themselves,

with their smiles painted on their cotton faces, that they thought everyone else should be cheerful too. And their friendly hugs and gentle voices did comfort the Hobby Horse enough for him to be able, between his sobs, to tell them his story.

"I have run away from Banzan the Magician, who made me. Banzan is able to make many things, but he is not a kind man. He has made me do whatever he wants and he beats me with a long willow switch when I tell him he is doing things that are wrong."

Then the Hobby Horse broke into tears and sobs again, and he could not go on until Raggedy Ann had wiped the tears away and comforted him once more.

Then he said, "I do not want to live with Banzan any longer, but he is chasing me even now, I am sure. And he will take me home with him and beat me again. Please help me, whoever you are, for you seem kind and gentle."

Raggedy Ann laughed. "Of course we will help you. I am Raggedy Ann and—" she turned to Raggedy Andy—"this is my dear friend Raggedy Andy.

We shall not let Banzan get you, you may be sure. Isn't that right, Raggedy Andy?"

Raggedy Andy agreed. "We are your friends, Hobby Horse, and we shall protect you."

The little redbird overhead, who had been watching and listening, chirped again. "Watch out, watch out! Here is a mean-looking creature running up the path."

Just in time the Raggedys pulled the Hobby Horse off the path and under the giant maple tree. Here, running up the path, came Banzan the Magician, huffing and puffing, barely able to catch his breath, "Aha! There you are, you wicked little Hobby Horse! What do you mean by running away from me? I have made you and you are supposed to do what I tell you to do," he called.

Before the Hobby Horse or the Raggedys could even think of an answer, Banzan went on yelling, "If you don't come here right away, I shall beat you again."

Now Raggedy Ann stepped forward and said, "Raggedy Andy and I will not let you beat the poor Hobby Horse. It is true you have made him, but he does not like the mean things you do to others, and he does not want to live with you any more." And Raggedy Andy joined in, "Why don't you just go home and leave the Hobby Horse alone?"

But Banzan would not give up so easily. By now he was cross as a bear, for he had grown hot and tired from chasing after the Hobby Horse. Every time he stepped closer to the group under the maple tree, and reached out to grab the Hobby Horse's reins, the Raggedys pushed the Hobby Horse farther away from him.

But he knew the Raggedys were not afraid of him and that he must think of a way to trick them. Although he tried hard, he could not think hard enough or fast enough. Really, Banzan the Magician was not a very good thinker anyway, for he was so used to doing things by magic that he did not bother to think much.

Banzan reached up into the boughs of the maple tree to get a switch so he might beat the Raggedys. But the kindly old maple tree held fast to all his limbs and would not let Banzan pull any off. When Banzan saw that the tree was stronger than he was, he looked all around until he finally found a stout stick on the ground.

"Aha!" he cried. "This will make you change your mind, I am sure." And he walked closer to the Raggedys. "If you do not let go of my Hobby Horse so he can come home with me, I shall beat both of you."

"Ha, Ha," laughed Raggedy Andy. "You cannot hurt my cotton stuffed body with that stick. But if you do not leave the Hobby Horse alone, the woodland creatures will take care of you."

You see, Raggedy Andy knew that the little redbird overhead had been chirping a message to all their woodland friends.

Suddenly, from all parts of the forest a troop of good little woodland creatures came marching. There was Berty Bear, Grampy Groundhog, Felix Fox, Walt Woodchuck and many, many other friends of the Raggedys.

Before he knew what had happened, Banzan the Magician was surrounded by the furry little animals. They were all good creatures who would not hurt anyone that did not try to hurt them or their friends. So they quietly waited for the Raggedys to tell them what to do.

Banzan was not happy to see all these creatures, and he decided he had better use some magic. Of course, he did not even try to figure out what was the best thing to do.

WORTH GRUELLE

As he said the magic words, *"Skippety-skip, trip-pety-trip,* now you are a magic stick! Magic stick, beat upon the woodland animals!" he raised the stick in the air.

He waited for the stick to beat Felix Fox and Walt Woodchuck and Grampy Groundhog and Berty Bear and all the others. But nothing happened. His magic was not strong enough against the goodness of the Raggedys and their friends.

The Hobby Horse neighed with pleasure, and Raggedy Ann said, "I think you had better go home, Banzan. Maybe when you decide to do good, happy things for others, your magic will be stronger."

Banzan did not know what to do. Making one last try, he swung his stick at Raggedy Ann, but before it could hit her, the little redbird flew down from the tree and knocked it out of his hand.

Banzan, knowing that his magic had failed him, slowly turned to go to his house in the wood. But just to make sure he would not ever bother the Hobby Horse and the Raggedys again, all the wood-land creatures marched behind him.

"From now on, I shall belong to you," the Hobby Horse told Raggedy Ann and Raggedy Andy. "For even if Banzan did make me with his magic, this a free country and I can belong to whomever I like best."

"We are very glad that you like us as much as you do, Hobby Horse," Raggedy Ann said. "You will find that we will always like you, too."

The Hobby Horse was so happy that he wanted

12

to do something nice for the Raggedys. He asked, "Wouldn't you like to go for a ride through the woods? I shall be glad to take you wherever you want to go."

"Why, thank you, Hobby Horse," the Raggedys said as they climbed up on the horse's back.

"Don't you get tired running so long, Hobby Horse?" Raggedy Andy asked, after they had traveled a long, long way on the Hobby Horse's back.

"Oh, no," the Hobby Horse replied without slowing up a bit. "You see, I am made entirely of wood and I never get tired at all. Why, I think I could run clear around the world without stopping once because I was tired!"

"That is a nice way to be," Raggedy Ann said. "Now, I can run a long way, but then I get tired and have to stop and rest, especially when I get hungry and thirsty."

"I never have been hungry or thirsty! I would like to taste something sometime," said the Hobby Horse wistfully.

"Just you take us to a nice ice-cream soda fountain or spring and we will show you how to drink ice-cream sodas," Raggedy Andy said.

So the Hobby Horse, because he was a magic Hobby Horse, knew just which way to go to find a lovely ice cream soda spring, and in two minutes the Raggedys slid from the Hobby Horse's back and were dipping up ice cream sodas.

"But how can we give the kind Hobby Horse ice cream sodas when he hasn't any mouth?" Raggedy Andy asked.

"Dear me! That's so!" Raggedy Ann said. "Why didn't Banzan the Magician give you a mouth?" she asked the Hobby Horse.

"I suppose because he thought he might have to feed me," the Hobby Horse answered.

Raggedy Andy looked closely at the Hobby Horse's head. "Do you know what, Raggedy Ann?" Raggedy Andy said. "It looks as if there is a knot right where the Hobby Horse's mouth is painted."

"There is," the Hobby Horse declared. "Once the knot came out and old Banzan glued it back."

"Ha, I thought so!" Raggedy Andy said as he took his whittling knife from his pocket. "It won't hurt you if I cut around the knot, will it?"

"No, not a bit," the Hobby Horse replied.

So Raggedy Andy pried around the knot with the smallest blade of his whittling knife and in a few moments he was able to pull the knot right out.

"Why," he cried, "it makes a dandy mouth, though it isn't very large."

"I can feel the air whistling in." The Hobby Horse laughed.

Raggedy Ann picked a nice round straw, placed it in a glass of soda and told the Hobby Horse how to drink.

"Whee!" the horse whistled through the knothole mouth. "It is the nicest soda I have ever tasted."

And his new friends laughed, because it was the first soda he had ever tasted. But they were very happy that such a good friend was able to share in their pleasures. For when we share our pleasures with others, it is always more fun for us.

"I know where there is a lovely cooky field," the

Hobby Horse said, "and it won't take me very long to carry you there if you like cookies."

"Then let us go there, nice Hobby Horse," Raggedy Ann said. "I am sure we would like some good cookies."

The wooden Hobby Horse was right: it took only three minutes to run to the cooky field which was the largest one the Raggedys had ever seen. All the cookies grew on short stems like dandelion blossoms, except that the cookies were quite large. And, since they were covered with frosting of different flavors and colors, they made a very pretty sight.

The Hobby Horse had hardly come to a stop before the Raggedys jumped from his back and began picking cookies.

"Are the cookies good?" asked the Hobby Horse.

"Very good!" Raggedy Ann replied as she broke cookies into small pieces and stuffed them into the Hobby Horse's mouth for him.

"When we have rested a bit, I shall enlarge the hole for the Hobby Horse's mouth," Raggedy Andy

16

said; "then he will be able to eat large pieces and everything else, just as we do."

After a while, Raggedy Andy took out his whittling knife and made the hole for the Hobby Horse's mouth large enough for him to eat whatever horses usually do.

Everyone was very happy then, and they decided to romp through the forest. Soon they came to a fork in the road, and the Raggedys and the Hobby Horse wondered which branch to take.

"I know what would be fun," suggested the Hobby Horse. "Since it looks as though both branches meet at the hilltop ahead, I shall take one fork of the road, and you Raggedys can take the other, and we shall see who gets there first!"

The Raggedys too thought that this sounded like fun. So, after throwing the Hobby Horse some kisses, they said good-by.

CHAPTER 2

THE RAGGEDYS went skipping along the path in the green forest. Every once in a while they would catch a glimpse of the Hobby Horse trotting along on the other side of the trees.

Many times they called, "Hello, Hobby Horse!" and each time he answered them in his cheery neigh. Finally the roads grew so far apart that they could not even see the tail of the Hobby Horse going by, and he did not answer their calls.

At last they came to the hilltop where the two roads met, but the Hobby Horse was not in sight. Thinking that he must have grown tired and stopped for a nap, they too sat under the shade of a tree and dozed a bit.

When they woke up, the Hobby Horse still had not arrived, and Raggedy Ann said, "Perhaps something has happened to the Hobby Horse, although I cannot imagine what it might be. Let's walk down the path that he took and see if we can find him."

Raggedy Andy, who felt uneasy, suggested, "He might have tripped and fallen. Or maybe he ate too many cookies and did not feel well."

As the Raggedys walked along, they searched for the Hobby Horse's footprints in the ground. But they could see none until they had gone about half-way back to their starting point. Then the Hobby Horse's four footprints were very plain indeed.

But the footprints just disappeared suddenly as though the Hobby Horse had been lifted into the air!

"This is very funny indeed," said Raggedy Andy in a troubled voice. "Where could the Hobby Horse have gone?"

They looked up into the trees, but no Hobby Horse was there of course.

At last Raggedy Ann said, "We must go back to the place where we said we would meet the Hobby Horse just in case he gets there somehow."

So the two Raggedys walked back, hand in hand, feeling very unhappy that they had lost their new friend.

Just as they reached their meeting place, the Hobby Horse came walking out of the bushes near by!

"Why, where have you been?" cried Raggedy Ann.

"It is a long story, Raggedy Ann," answered the Hobby Horse in a tired voice. "But I am very thirsty, so let's find a nice soda-water fountain, and then I will tell you all about it."

"Now, Hobby Horse, please tell us where you have been all this time," Raggedy Ann said as she and

Raggedy Andy and the Hobby Horse came to a beautiful woodland ice-cream-soda spring.

"Well," the Hobby Horse said after he had taken a drink of strawberry ice-cream soda, "I do not know just how I happened to get away from you, Raggedys, but I believe I must have had some magic worked on me. Anyway, I seemed to awaken from a nap, and I was shut up in a dark barn."

At this point, the Hobby Horse took a long drink of strawberry-ice-cream soda.

Then he continued: "I knew it was a barn because when I started to run I went smack into a wooden wall and bumped my head. Then I ran the other way and bumped against the other side. I guess I made a lot of noise, for soon a door opened and a little old lady poked her head in and said, 'My goodness! What in the world are you trying to do?"

" 'I'm trying to get out of here,' I told her.

" 'Don't you know that you can't run right through the side of a wooden barn?' she asked me.

" 'Yes,' I replied. 'But how was I to know that I was in a wooden barn when I couldn't see?'

"The little old lady laughed and patted me on the head. 'Of course, there was no way for you to know,' she said. Then she told me to come into the house with her and she would see if she could find some sawdust for me. And into the house I went!"

"She must have been a very kindly old lady," Raggedy Ann said.

The Hobby Horse chuckled to himself, then said aloud, "Indeed she was, Raggedy Ann, and when I told her that I would like something besides sawdust food, she gave me some doughnuts and cookies. Then she told me that she had found me lying in the path near her house. She and her husband had carried me into the barn.

" 'We thought you were just a play Hobby Horse,' she told me.

"She said that her husband had hardly locked the door to the barn when a queer little man came running up and asked, 'Where did you put that magical Hobby Horse? Tell me quick or I shall change you both into Willywiggles!'

"So they knew that the queer little man was a Wiz-

ard. Still, he was so impolite, the little old lady said to him, 'If that was your Hobby Horse, why did you leave him lying in the path?'

"And the Wizard howled and said, 'Just because! That's why!'

" 'Then I do not believe it is your Hobby Horse at all,' the kind little old lady said.

"This made the Wizard very angry and he poked his stick at the little old lady and said, 'You must become a Willywiggle!' But the little lady had her fingers crossed and the magic did not work. So the Wizard did the same to the little old lady's kind husband and he changed right into a Willywiggle!

"The Wizard put a string around his neck and took him home. Of course, the little old lady was very, very unhappy. So I told her that I would find Raggedy Ann and Raggedy Andy and we would rescue the nice little old man from the impolite Wizard."

"And we shall go with you right away," cried Raggedy Andy. Jumping to their feet, Raggedy Ann and Raggedy Andy followed the Hobby Horse through the woods.

"Let's see," the magical Hobby Horse said as he came to a stop where three paths led away from the main road. "I have forgotten which way I came. It was dark when I left the kind little old lady's house to find you."

"Then I think you should be blindfolded," Raggedy Ann said to the Hobby Horse. "If you could not see when you came down one of these paths, of course you would not remember which one it was, now that you can see."

She tied her hanky around the Hobby Horse's head so that his knothole eyes were completely covered.

"How is that, wooden Hobby Horse?" she asked.

"That is just right, Raggedy Ann," the Hobby Horse replied. "I can tell now that it was the right-

hand path; so we will walk down it." The magical Hobby Horse walked down the right-hand path and the Raggedys followed him until he came to a queer little house.

"Hmmm," Raggedy Ann said as she caught hold of the Hobby Horse's tail. "I do believe that you have taken the wrong path, Mr. Hobby Horse!"

"Why do you say that, Raggedy Ann?" the Hobby Horse asked.

"Because," Raggedy Ann answered, "this queer house is such a funny little place that I am sure no nice litle old lady lives here!"

"Please take your hanky from my eyes," the Hobby Horse said, and when he could see, the Hobby Horse agreed. "Well, you are right! I *have* come the wrong way!"

"No, you haven't," a squeaky voice in the bushes said. And there stood the strangest creature the Raggedys had ever seen!

"My goodness!" the wooden Hobby Horse cried as he jumped to one side. "What kind of a creature are you?"

At this, the strange creature began crying, and Raggedy Ann had to wipe his eyes three times with her hanky before he could speak.

"I am a Willywiggle!" he sighed. "But I have been a Willywiggle only a short time and it was because of that wooden Hobby Horse there that the impolite Wizard changed me into a Willywiggle. I can tell you it isn't any fun being a Willywiggle and looking this way. And besides, I have to eat hay and old dried corncobs."

"Indeed, I'm sure it isn't fun!" Raggedy Andy agreed soothingly.

Raggedy Ann said, "And it is just because the impolite Wizard changed you into a Willywiggle that we are here; for we have come to rescue you if we can."

"I imagine that you can rescue me easily enough," the Willywiggle said. "But how can you change me into a man again? That's what I would like to know."

"And that is what we must try to find out from the impolite Wizard," Raggedy Ann said.

"I have an idea!" said Raggedy Andy. "Suppose

I go to the impolite Wizard's house and get a job as his housemaid. Maybe I can find out how he works his magic and then we shall change the Willywiggle back into a man."

This seemed a good idea to everyone. So Raggedy Andy, while his friends hid in the bushes where they could watch, ran up to the queer little house and knocked at the door.

"Who is knocking at my door?" the impolite Wizard asked.

Raggedy Andy knocked again, and the Wizard came to the door and asked, "What do you want?"

"I have come to be a housemaid," Raggedy Andy said. "No charge for services."

"But I do not want a housemaid," yelled the Wizard.

"But if you had a housemaid, then she could do all the work around the house and help you with your magic," Raggedy Andy said.

"I believe you are trying to fool me," the Wizard said. "How can you be a housemaid when you don't charge anything for doing the work?"

"Because," Raggedy Andy replied, "if I were really and truly a housemaid, you would have to pay me, or I wouldn't be hired; but I am Raggedy Andy and a boy, so I can be a housemaid as easy as pie without getting paid. Now don't you see?"

"Hmmm, I don't see!" the Wizard said. "But come in anyway, and if I find out that you are trying to fool me, I shall very soon change you into something you do not wish to be!"

When Raggedy Andy went into the Wizard's house he looked all about to make sure the Wizard did not have any magic lying around loose. Then he asked, "What would you like for me to cook for breakfast, Mr. Wizard?"

"See here," the Wizard cried as he put on his glasses and looked sharply at Raggedy Andy. "I have not yet had supper. Why should you want to know what I want for breakfast?"

"Because I shall start work tomorrow," Raggedy Andy replied. "And I shall have to start your breakfast before you are awake."

"Indeed! You must start work right away. You will have to cook supper now because I am hungry."

"Oh well, all right!" Raggedy Andy agreed. "Have you any lopdoosies? I shall fry some for your supper. Or I shall bake some flapdoodles to have with stewed clicks."

The Wizard scratched his head a moment. Then he reached for his magic stick. "I shall just see if you are trying to fool me," he said.

"I have never heard of those things at all, and I do not believe there are any things like lopdoosies and flapdoodles and clicks!" He was just about to point his magic stick at Raggedy Andy when the rag doll said, "Excuse me, Mr. Wizard, please. Did you ever hear that there were no flapdoodles?"

"Of course not, silly!" the Wizard said. "If I had heard that there were no flapdoodles, then I would not have to work magic to find out."

"Then save your magic for another time," Rag-

28

gedy Andy advised. "I can show you flapdoodles in a few minutes."

So the Wizard rocked in his rocking chair while Raggedy Andy prepared the flapdoodles. Raggedy Andy mixed some flour and water until it made a ball of dough. When this was quite thick, he took the pan of dough and, holding it close to the Wizard's face, he said, "Now, whistle three times!"

When the Wizard had whistled three times, Raggedy Andy turned the pan of dough upside down on the Wizard's head! And as the Wizard scrambled around trying to get the sticky dough out of his eyes and nose, Raggedy Andy quickly took the magic stick and ran out of the house.

"Now we shall soon change the Willywiggle back into a nice old man!" Raggedy Andy said to himself.

CHAPTER 3

FROM WHERE Raggedy Ann, Raggedy Andy, and
the magical Hobby Horse were hiding in the bushes,
they could hear the impolite Wizard screaming and
howling.

"What in the world did you do to him?" Raggedy
Ann asked Raggedy Andy.

"I fooled him, that's what!" Raggedy Andy
answered as he showed his friends the Wizard's
magic stick which he had taken. "I made some flapdoodles for the Wizard and when I had flour and
water mixed up into a sticky dough, I put the pan of
dough on the Wizard's head. That's why he is
screaming!"

"But it was wrong for you to take the Wizard's
magic stick, Raggedy Andy," Raggedy Ann said.

"I know that, Raggedy Ann," Raggedy Andy replied. "But I have only borrowed it for a few minutes so that I may use it to change the Willywiggle
back into a nice old man again. You see, it was very

wrong for the Wizard to change the nice old man into a Willywiggle!"

"My goodness, where is the Willywiggle now?" Raggedy Ann asked as she looked all about her.

"Here I am," the Willywiggle said, taking his head out from under a fern. "I heard the Wizard screaming and howling and I thought maybe he was coming to work more magic on me. So I stuck my head under this fern to hide."

Raggedy Ann and Raggedy Andy could only laugh, for even with his head hidden, the Willywiggle's large body could still be seen.

"Now I shall take the Wizard's wand and change you back into a man," Raggedy Andy told the Willywiggle as he pointed the wand at the sad creature.

Raggedy Andy tapped the Willywiggle with the wand and said, *"Hokus-pokus!"* But the Willywiggle was still a Willywiggle. Raggedy Andy tried all the other magic words he could think of, but the Willywiggle did not change back into a man.

"Maybe the dry weather doesn't let the magic wand work," the wooden Hobby Horse said.

"Do you know what?" Raggedy Andy asked and then answered himself: "I do not believe the Wizard's wand is worth anything at all! It isn't even a magic stick. I shall take it right back to him."

And Raggedy Andy ran back to the Wizard who was trying to wash the dough off his face, and said, "Here's your magic wand, Mister Wizard. I'm sorry that I borrowed it. I guess it isn't really a magic wand at all."

31

"Ha!" the Wizard cried when he saw Raggedy Andy. "I suspected that you were trying to fool me when you told me you wanted to be my housemaid. So I made a magic wish that the wand would not work if you were fooling me. Now, just as soon as I finish washing my face, I shall work magic on *you!* I shall change you into a Willywiggle, that's what I shall do! Then you will be mighty sorry that you tried to fool me."

"Hmm," Raggedy Andy thought to himself, "I guess I'd better not stay here and be changed into a Willywiggle, because the Willywiggles are funny-looking creatures. And, if I am a Willywiggle, I shall not be able to help change the Willywiggle who is outside into a man."

So Raggedy Andy left the Wizard washing his face and ran to Raggedy Ann and the others.

"We must hurry," Raggedy Andy told them as he helped Raggedy Ann onto the Hobby Horse, "for the Wizard will be after us in a few minutes."

As the Hobby Horse ran down the path through the deep, deep woods, the unhappy Willywiggle ran alongside.

"Oh dear," the funny-looking Willywiggle said as he came to a stop, "I cannot run any further! I am not used to being a Willywiggle and I cannot keep up with you."

And of course, when the Willywiggle stopped running, Raggedy Andy and the wooden Hobby Horse stopped running too; for they did not wish to run on and leave the poor Willywiggle all alone.

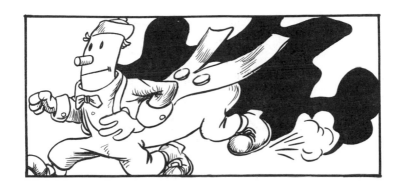

"I really think you had better run along and leave me," the Willywiggle said. "If the Wizard catches up with us, I am sure that he will change all of you into Willywiggles. And Willywiggles cannot have any fun. I would much rather be a man as I used to be."

"And that is why we shall stay with you, instead of leaving you behind," Raggedy Ann said as she jumped from the back of the wooden Hobby Horse. "We shall try to make the Wizard change you back into a man again, so that you may go back to your nice, kind wife."

"Oh, thank you!" exclaimed the Willywiggle, brushing the tears from his eyes. "Maybe I can help *you* some day."

"Anyway," the Hobby Horse said, "the Wizard is coming, I am sure. I hear something thumping on the ground. It sounds as though he must be on a horse."

"Let us all hide in these thick bushes," Raggedy Ann said. "Then perhaps the Wizard will not see us."

So they hid in the bushes, and pretty soon along came the Wizard riding on a wooden horse. His horse looked something like Raggedy Ann's magical wooden Hobby Horse, but he was not so handsome.

"They are right around here," the Wizard's horse said as he came to a stop.

"What did you want to tell for?" Raggedy Ann asked as she came out of the bushes. "It isn't a bit fair if someone tells where we are hiding."

"Of course it is," the Wizard cried. "Why do you think I made a magical wooden horse if he can't help me chase you and tell me where you are hidden. Just tell me that!"

"Anyway, it isn't fair," Raggedy Ann said, "because we did not yell 'ready!'"

"How can you say such silly things?" the Wizard screamed. He was much annoyed now. "I came to capture you, not to play games with you!"

"Then if you are not playing 'I spy' we will not play with you," Raggedy Ann said. "So you can just turn around and run back home."

And before the Wizard could think of a reply to

make, his wooden horse turned around and carried the Wizard right back home.

"Ha, ha, ha!" the Willywiggle laughed. "Raggedy Ann fooled the old silly that time!"

Since there was a lollypop tree right in back of the bushes where they had all been hidden, the Raggedys, the Willywiggle and the magical Hobby Horse went to pick some lollypops off the tree.

Naturally, after eating many lollypops they needed a drink. So the wooden Hobby Horse led the way to a fine orange drink fountain which bubbled up from between some pretty colored rocks.

When they were no longer thirsty, the wooden Hobby Horse said, "This is a lovely place to hide, for the ice-cold orange drink fountain is delicious and we are quite near the lollypop tree too. But I think the Wizard will be coming back in a few minutes on his wooden horse."

"The Wizard's wooden horse looks so much like you that he could be your brother, if wooden Hobby horses had brothers," Raggedy Andy said.

"Maybe he was made with the same magic that

made me," the Hobby Horse said. "Anyway, we must hurry and run along through the woods so the Wizard will not change you into Willywiggles as he did this poor Willywiggle. Are you ready?"

"All ready!" Raggedy Ann cried as she climbed onto the Hobby Horse's back.

"Since the Willywiggle gets too tired when he runs and cannot keep up with the Hobby Horse," Raggedy Andy said, "I will have to carry him." And, picking up the Willywiggle, Raggedy Andy set off beside the magical Hobby Horse. To his surprise, he found that the Willywiggle was as light as a bag of feathers.

The magical Hobby Horse and Raggedy Andy ran as fast as they could. Finally, when Raggedy Andy was out of breath, they came to a stop.

"I think we have gone far enough now so the Wizard will not find us," Raggedy Ann said. Looking around, she found that they had stopped beside a pancake stone. This made everyone happy, for they were hungry. Now the pancake stone was a very unusual one: it baked pancakes while you waited beside it. The pancake batter was in a large pitcher hanging from the limb of a tree, above the hot stone, and when the batter dropped down upon the stone, the pancakes cooked all by themselves. Then, when they were done on one side, they flipped over onto the other side and then into a pan of butter.

So the Raggedys and their friends took the pancakes from the butter pan, dipped them in a syrup puddle and then ate them.

While they were doing this, the Wizard appeared, crying, "Aha! Now I have you, because a while ago, I heard Raggedy Ann yell, 'All ready!'"

"But I was not playing games then," Raggedy Ann said. "I was answering the Hobby Horse."

"Anyway, now that I have captured you, I shall change you all into Willywiggles!" exclaimed the Wizard, who was taking all his magic charms from his pocket. And he would have changed them all into Willywiggles if Raggedy Andy had not caught one of the pancakes and thrown it onto the Wizard's long nose.

Since the pancake was cooked only on one side, the uncooked side stuck fast. With a loud howl the Wizard dashed down the path in search of a brook in which to put his nose to cool it off.

While he was doing this, the Raggedys and the Willywiggle hopped upon the magical Hobby Horse who ran away faster than he had ever thought he could run.

The mean old Wizard was very angry with Raggedy Andy for putting the hot pancake on his nose.

So as soon as he had cooled his nose off in a brook near by, he hopped on his wooden hobby horse and started off to find the Raggedys, the Willywiggle, and the magical Hobby Horse.

"Ha, just wait until I catch them!" the Wizard screamed as he rode through the deep, deep woods lickety-split. "I will change them into Willywiggles all right."

And so the Wizard went galloping through the woods, and because his hobby horse knew just which way the Raggedys had gone, in a short time the Wizard could see them running down the path ahead of him.

Because Raggedy Ann's Hobby Horse was carrying more people than the Wizard's, he could not run so fast. The Wizard's hobby horse came closer and closer. Soon the Wizard was so close he was able to reach over and pull Raggedy Andy from Raggedy Ann's Hobby Horse. But what he did not know was that Raggedy Andy would fight with him when he did this.

Raggedy Andy immediately threw his rag arms around the Wizard's neck and wrapped his legs around the front legs of the Wizard's hobby horse. This tripped the hobby horse who fell head over heels, throwing Raggedy Andy and the Wizard far to one side.

Of course the fall did not hurt Raggedy Andy a bit, for he was made of cloth and stuffed with soft cotton. But the Wizard hit his head on a stone and soon had a large bump on his head.

But this did not stop Raggedy Andy. He kept right on fighting the Wizard and allowed him to sit up.

"Maybe after this you will know that it's not a good idea to try to capture us," Raggedy Ann told the Wizard. "Raggedy Andy is a very strong fighter and he could have hurt you much more."

And the Wizard said, "My goodness, if I had known Raggedy Andy was such a strong fighter, I never would have tried to change any of you into Willywiggles or anything else!"

Getting on his hobby horse, he went back the way he had come.

Raggedy Ann sighed and said, "Thank goodness, he has gone!" But then she heard the Willywiggle sobbing and, turning to him in surprise, she asked, "Why, whatever is the matter? Aren't you glad to see the Wizard go?"

"I wish that while Raggedy Andy was fighting the Wizard he had made the Wizard promise to change me back into a man," the Willywiggle said as the tears streamed down his funny cheeks.

39

"Why ever didn't someone think of it?" Raggedy Andy asked. "It would have been so easy!"

"Maybe we can catch up with the Wizard and make him do it even now," the Willywiggle said.

"That is a fine idea, Willywiggle," Raggedy Ann said. "Let's all get on the Hobby Horse and follow the Wizard. Then when we catch up with him, Raggedy Andy can tell him he will fight him unless he changes the Willywiggle back into a man again."

"But I cannot carry all of you as fast as the Wizard's hobby horse can carry him," Raggedy Ann's magical Hobby Horse said. "Let me take Raggedy Andy on my back and when I catch up with the Wizard, Raggedy Andy can make him come back with us and work his magic on the Willywiggle!"

Raggedy Ann thought this was a good idea, and since there was a chocolate-cooky bush growing close by, she and the Willywiggle had some cookies while Raggedy Andy and the Hobby Horse ran after the Wizard.

In a very short time Raggedy Andy could see the Wizard riding on his hobby horse through the woods and in a few minutes he had caught up with him.

"We forgot something, Mr. Wizard," Raggedy Andy said politely.

"No sir! I haven't forgotten a single thing," the Wizard replied as he rubbed the bump on top of his head. "I will never fight with you again, Raggedy Andy, that is certain!"

"Will you please come back with me and change the Willywiggle into a man again so that he can return to his nice wife?" Raggedy Andy asked.

"Oh no, I couldn't do that," the Wizard said. "You see, I have a very important engagement this afternoon."

"Then I guess we will have to fight again," Raggedy Andy said as he rolled up his sleeves.

"Wait, wait!" the Wizard screamed. "I guess I will go back with you after all, Raggedy Andy, because I have had enough fighting to last me for several days."

So he turned his hobby horse around and, with Raggedy Andy close beside him to see that he did not try to run away, they went back down the path to the others.

"Now the Wizard will change the Willywiggle back into a man again," Raggedy Andy said as he and the Wizard rode up to Raggedy Ann and the Willywiggle.

The Wizard still thought there was some way he could escape, and he searched for it all through the woods, but with Raggedy Andy on one side of him and Raggedy Ann on the other, he knew he could not.

"Well, I guess, if there is no other way, I will have to do it," said the Wizard, "but I would rather not. You see, when I change the Willywiggle back to a man he will probably scream awfully loud, for Willywiggles always do that."

"And I guess he will not do anything of the kind," Raggedy Ann said to the Wizard. "Don't you know it's wrong to tell lies, Mr. Wizard?"

"All right! You just wait and see," the Wizard

answered, "but do not blame me if the Willywiggle howls awfully."

"Maybe I had better stay a Willywiggle," the Willywiggle said to Raggedy Ann. "Perhaps it will hurt if I am going to scream awfully."

"Oh, you can't imagine how loudly he will scream!" the Wizard said.

"Now see here," Raggedy Ann said, shaking her hand under the Wizard's long nose. "It is very wrong of you to frighten the poor Willywiggle. And I'm very sure that it won't hurt him a tiny bit."

"Maybe my magic isn't working well today because of the dry weather," the Wizard said. "I guess I'll wait until tomorrow." And he started to ride away through the woods.

But Raggedy Andy caught the Wizard's arm and pulled him from the wooden hobby horse and acted as though he would start to fight.

This frightened the Wizard because he knew Raggedy Andy could beat him easily, so he cried, "All right. I'll change the Willywiggle back into a man!"

The Wizard got out all his magic charms and his

magic wand too. Placing the wand on the Willywiggle's head, he closed his eyes and called out: "Allakazan, allakazoo! Allakazoo, allakazan! Willywiggle, change into a man!"

The Raggedys and the Hobby Horse were watching closely to make sure the Wizard did not play any tricks on them, but, sure enough right before their eyes, the Willywiggle became a nice old man.

And Raggedy Ann had been right of course, because the Willywiggle did not even squeak, let alone howl or yell as the Wizard had said he would.

The little old man was so happy that he hugged the Raggedys and the Magical Hobby Horse, and almost hugged the Wizard. He could not wait to get back to his dear little wife, so Raggedy Ann suggested that they all ride back with him.

When they got back to where the kindly little old lady had been waiting, the nice little old man hugged his wife ever so many times, and everyone was very happy.

"It is a shame for the Wizard to work such unkind magic," Raggedy Ann said. "Maybe it would be a

good idea to take all the magic charms away from him so that he can never do any mean magic again."

But the Wizard begged, "If you will let me have my charms, I promise I will never work unkind magic again."

"But how can we be sure that you mean what you say?" Raggedy Ann asked.

"I don't know," the Wizard replied, "but if you take all my charms from me, I will not be able to have any fun."

"Just let me see your magic charms, Mr. Wizard, please," Raggedy Ann said, as she held out her hand.

So the Wizard turned over the bag in which he kept his magic charms and they fell into Raggedy Ann's hand.

"Well, no wonder!" Raggedy Ann cried as she looked at the charms. "Just look at these things, Raggedy Andy!"

The wooden Hobby Horse peeked over Raggedy Andy's shoulder so he might see too. There was a carpet tack, the cork out of a little pill bottle, two red buttons and a hairpin.

"Just look at that!" Raggedy Ann said. "How can anyone expect to work nice, kindly magic when one of the charms is a crooked carpet tack and another is a twisted hairpin? Just tell me, Mr. Wizard, how did you expect that?"

"I never thought of it," the Wizard replied, as he kicked his toes in the sand and hung his head. "I picked up the charms along the path here in the woods and thought they might be magic charms, and when I tried them, they worked—just like magic!"

So the nice little old man straightened out the carpet tack and the hairpin, and then Raggedy Ann handed the charms back to the Wizard.

"Now try them, Mr. Wizard," Raggedy Andy suggested.

The Wizard made a wish, and everyone was delighted to see a patch of fruits of all kinds and colors growing right beside a cherry soda fountain!

"Whee!" Raggedy Ann exclaimed. "Now I'm sure you'll have much more fun working magic than you did before."

"I'm sure that I shall." The Wizard laughed. "I am sorry now that I changed the nice little old man into a Willywiggle and was so unpleasant to everyone."

The little old man whispered something to his nice little wife, and then he said, "Mr. Wizard, now that you are happy again and will make only nice magic, my wife and I would like to invite you to come live with us."

The Wizard was so surprised that he did not know what to say at first, but then he exclaimed, "Thank you, thank you! You are very kind to me after the way I treated you. And I shall gladly stay with you so that I may make up for the unkind things I did."

Everyone sat down then to have some delicious sweet fruit and soda, and Raggedy Ann said, "Now I think Raggedy Andy and the magical Hobby Horse and I must go on to look for more adventures." And off they rode into the woods.

CHAPTER 4

BEFORE THE MAGICAL Hobby Horse had galloped many steps, the Raggedys could hear the Wizard calling after them, "Raggedy Ann, Raggedy Andy, you Raggedys, come back, come back!"

Wondering what the trouble could be, the Hobby Horse turned around sharply and doubled his speed. As he arrived, he called out breathlessly, "What is it? What's happened?"

The nice little old man and his dear wife wore big smiles on their round, happy faces. And the Wizard's eyes twinkled as though he knew something very special.

He explained to the Raggedys and to the Hobby Horse, "After you left, I had an idea. I thought to myself that it would be nice if I did something with my good magic for you. What would you like me to make?"

The Hobby Horse and the Raggedys thought for a long time and then Raggedy Ann said, "We have

never been on a boat, Mr. Wizard. Could you wish a magical boat for us?"

But before the Wizard could answer, Raggedy Andy added, "Maybe you'd better wish for a Captain too, because we would not know how to make a boat go."

The Hobby Horse stamped his feet excitedly and said, "That is a grand idea! But what is a boat? I do not think I have ever seen one!"

Everyone laughed and then the Wizard took out all his magic charms and even his magic wand.

He closed his eyes and said the magic words, "Allakazan, Allakazoo! Allakazoo, Allakazan! I want a little white boat for her friends and Raggedy Ann! Allakazan, Allakazoo! Allakazoo, Allakazan! I wish for a little Captain to steer the magical white boat!"

And there right in front of them stood a jolly, fat little Captain in a white suit and hat with shiny brass buttons!

The jolly fat little Captain smiled and greeted them, "It is good to meet my new passengers. I hope we will have a good cruise together."

Raggedy Ann cried, "But there is no boat! How can we have a cruise?"

And everyone but the Wizard and the Captain searched the bushes around them, looking for a little white boat. The Captain and the Wizard laughed and laughed till they hardly could speak.

Finally the Wizard said, "Naturally the boat would not be here. It must be in the water! If you will all walk down the path to the river, you will find your boat."

So once more the Raggedys and Hobby Horse said good-by to the Wizard and the nice little old man and his sweet wife. And they walked down the path through the deep, deep woods until they came to the little magic boat. It was a wonderful little white cruiser which rested at the river's edge. It shone in the sunlight and looked sturdy enough to take them anywhere.

The magical Hobby Horse said, "That is the first boat I have ever seen, but I am sure it is the most beautiful boat there is!"

So the Raggedys, the Hobby Horse, and the little

fat captain went aboard and the pretty white magic boat glided out over the smooth waters of the river.

"We will just let the little white magic boat sail in any direction it wishes." The little Captain laughed. "Then we shall be surprised when we sail into an adventure!"

When Raggedy Andy went into the cabin, he found a surprise there: a magic cupboard and a magic soda fountain! He saw some cream puffs and ice-cream cones waiting and decided to take them out to the others right away so they might sit on the deck and enjoy the goodies.

Just as everyone had finished eating all the cream puffs and ice cream cones, and when Raggedy Andy had started into the cabin for more, they all heard a loud *"Boom!"* And then a cannon ball went skipping over the water ahead of the little white boat.

"My gracious!" the little Captain cried. "We must stop. But who could be doing a thing like that?"

Raggedy Ann peeped around the corner of the cabin and exclaimed, "Ha! It's a great big boat with a black flag! Good gracious, that must mean Pirates!"

"That's just who they are," the little Captain cried as he viewed the large boat through spyglasses. "Real Pirates, not pretend pirates like the crew of my old boat. What shall we do? If they capture this fine little magical boat with its magical ice-cream fountain and magical cupboards and everything, the Pirates are sure to make us walk the plank!"

"Then I guess we will have to stop and fight them," Raggedy Andy said as he rolled up his sleeves.

"I can help with that," said the Hobby Horse.

"But we are only four," the little Captain said, "and that large boat has a great many Pirates on it, I imagine."

"There, they fired!" Raggedy Ann cried as another cannon ball skipped ahead of the little white boat. "Next time maybe they will hit our little boat and make a big hole in the side!"

"We had better stop," the little fat Captain said as he turned the magic switch to "STOP."

Presently the large boat came up beside the little boat, and the Pirates loaded a rowboat and put a ladder up to the magical boat. But just as they started to climb up the ladder, the little magical boat began wiggling from side to side ever so hard, and the Pirates tumbled into the sea.

Since there were no Pirates left on board the large boat who could fire at them, Raggedy Andy ran to the magic switch and turned it to "VERY FAST." Before the Pirates could swim to the rowboat and get aboard their large boat, the little magic white boat was just a tiny dot in the distance. And of course, a cannon ball could not go that far!

"Now we can finish eating." Raggedy Andy laughed as he brought more ice cream cones and cream puffs from the magic cupboard.

It was so pleasant riding up on the deck of the little white magic boat! Everything and everyone seemed so far away that none of the passengers thought anything unpleasant could happen. But suddenly the little boat began to whirl round and round and the sky became very dark.

"A storm must be blowing up," the little Captain cried to Raggedy Ann who could hardly hear him because the wind was howling so loud. As the little boat whirled round faster and faster, and water began falling all over the deck, and the boat seemed to rise out of the river, the Raggedys, the Hobby Horse and the little Captain went inside the cabin and closed the windows. When they had switched on the lamps and drawn the draperies, the cabin was so dry and cozy that it was hard to believe it was dark and stormy outside.

"This is the worst storm I have ever seen!" exclaimed the little Captain as he went to a magic instrument on the wall. This instrument told just what kind of weather the little boat could expect to sail into.

"My gracious!" the little Captain cried when he looked at the magical instrument. "We should have looked at this before. Just see here!"

And when the Raggedys and the Hobby Horse looked at the magical instrument they saw an indicator pointing to "WATERSPOUT."

"Dear me!" Raggedy Ann said. "A water spout! No wonder it grew so dark and so much water fell upon the deck and we've been lifted out of the river. What shall we do, Captain?"

"I am afraid there is nothing to do until the waterspout breaks and lets us down to the river again," the little Captain said.

"But what if it lets us drop so quickly and so hard that it smashes the little magic boat to pieces?" asked

the Hobby Horse in a trembling voice.

"Oh, I'm sure it won't do that," Raggedy Andy said. "This is a magic boat and I do not believe a waterspout could do that to it. Anyway, it will do no good to worry. So let's play some games or have the Captain read to us until the storm dies down."

So the Raggedys, the Hobby Horse and the little Captain played Tiddly-winks until suddenly there was a great big "BUMP," and the Raggedys and the little Captain and everything went rolling across the cabin. Only the Hobby Horse, who had four legs to stand on, did not lose his balance.

As Raggedy Ann got to her feet and looked out the window, she laughed. "Anyway, we are out of the waterspout. See, there it goes, 'way across there!"

And sure enough, they could see the giant waterspout traveling very fast across the water.

"Oh dear," the little fat Captain cried, "just look here!"

And when they all looked over the side of the little boat, they saw that it was stuck fast, right on the tip-top peak of a mountain.

The magic Hobby Horse thought quietly a minute and then said, "We must have sailed far out into the ocean, for there are no mountains near the river."

Raggedy Ann said, "You are quite right, Hobby Horse. It's a good thing this is a magical boat, for we have everything we can wish for to eat. So let's just have a lot of fun until we are rescued."

"The view is fine from up here," the little Captain said, "but I am afraid that after a day or so we will grow tired of staying on top of this mountain. And the little boat is made to sail on water. The sun may dry it out so much that the sides will warp and crack wide open."

"Maybe the Wizard made the little boat so it could

sail on the water or sail in the air," Raggedy Ann ventured.

"My goodness! I never heard of a boat that sailed in the air, except a balloon boat!" the little Captain said.

"That wouldn't make any difference. If the Wizard made it so it could sail either in the air or on the water, then that is what it will do," the Hobby Horse said. "Let's look over the boat carefully and see if we can find out whether it is only a water boat!"

So the four friends went to the magical switch and there they saw the words "UP" and "DOWN" as well as many other directions.

Raggedy Ann said, "We will just have to try! Move the switch, Captain, and maybe the boat will go down the mountain."

The little Captain moved the switch so that the pointer moved to "DOWN," but the little magical boat only crunched against the stone it rested on. It wiggled a bit, but nothing else happened.

"No," the little Captain said, "it is only a water boat after all, and we shall have to stay here all the

rest of our lives!" And then he began to cry very, very hard.

Raggedy Ann wiped the Captain's tears away with her apron and gave him two cream puffs and a doughnut before he could stop.

"We shall never, never get off this mountain top and be able to have any fun again!" the Captain said.

"Ah! You must not believe that, Captain," Raggedy Andy said, "for I am sure some day a flying boat will come along this way and rescue us. I wouldn't worry at all if I were you."

"Neither would I." Raggedy Ann laughed. "Raggedy Andy and I have been in lots of places worse than this, and each time we were rescued—weren't we, Raggedy Andy?"

"Every single time," Raggedy Andy answered. "Anyway," he said as he walked over and looked at the switch, "maybe when you turned the switch to 'DOWN' the magic boat was as far down as it could go, for it is resting right on top of a large mountain."

"Whee!" Raggedy Ann cried. "Raggedy Andy is right! You should have turned the switch to 'UP'!"

So, when the little Captain turned the switch to "UP," the little magic boat rose from the tiptop stone on the mountain and went sailing up and up, until Raggedy Ann turned the switch to "STRAIGHT AHEAD." Then the magical boat sailed swiftly through the air, high above the earth.

CHAPTER 5

"This is a very fine magical boat the Wizard has made for you, Captain," Raggedy Ann said as she, Raggedy Andy, and the Captain and the wooden Hobby Horse sat out on the deck eating cream puffs and drinking pink lemonade.

Far down below them they could see the lovely green of trees and grass, and little dots which they knew were houses. Great fleecy clouds just like masses of white cotton floated by them too.

But everything was so still with not another person around whom they could see or hear that it seemed very strange to all of them.

"Maybe we had better sail down to the earth again," the little fat Captain finally said. "It's so cold up here that the lemonade is freezing into ice! Let's sail back down to the earth. What do you say?"

"I think it would be more fun," Raggedy Ann agreed, "because there isn't much chance of having an adventure 'way up here!"

The little Captain was just about to turn the switch to "DOWN" when Raggedy Andy exclaimed, "Look there! Do you see that little spot 'way over there? Maybe it is a meteor!"

The little Captain got out his spy glass and looked at the speck. "My goodness!" he cried. "What do you suppose it is?" Then before they could guess, he said, "It is a man in a boat and he is waving his arms at us!"

"Maybe he has been shipwrecked from an airplane and he is trying to attract our attention so we may rescue him," Raggedy Andy said.

The little Captain turned the switch so that the little magical boat sailed right up to where the man sat in a tiny rowboat. The Captain and Raggedy Andy helped the sky sailor onto the magical white boat.

"Gracious!" the man said as he sat down in a chair. "That's the first time I've ever been shipwrecked 'way up in the air. I thought I would never be rescued. You know, it is very lonely 'way up here, miles above the earth without anyone to keep you com-

pany, and with nothing to eat or drink. I'm very glad you happened to sail by this way."

Raggedy Ann hastened into the cabin and soon returned with a large plate of hamburgers, a dish of ice cream, and two large glasses of lemonade. The sailor was very glad to see all this good food and, when he had finished eating every bit of it, he told them what had happened.

"I was sailing on a tugboat last night and had gone to sleep in my bunk when all of a sudden I felt the boat whirling round and round. I did not know what was wrong but very soon the captain told everyone to get into boats and pull for the shore. Before I knew it, everyone had piled into all the big boats and I was left all alone with this little tiny boat. I got into it and lowered it into the water. My, but it was dark and the wind howled and was so strong, it almost pushed me over. But I snuggled down into the little boat and I was so tired that I just fell asleep.

"But this morning when I awakened, there I was, 'way up in the middle of the air, and I think I must still be dreaming. But how did you get into my dream?"

The wooden Hobby Horse laughed and told the weary sailor, "No, we are not dreams, my friends and I! And I will pinch you to show you that you are awake."

When he had gently pinched the sailor, who did not even have to say "Ouch!" the Hobby Horse told him that they too had been in a waterspout and had gone round and round.

The little Captain said, "You must have been in the same waterspout we were in. Now that we have rescued you, you must promise to stay with us until we reach the earth again."

"Oh, I will gladly promise that!" the sailor said as he looked down over the side of the boat. "It must be miles down there and I do not think I would like to jump that far."

The little fat Captain set the switch again so that it pointed to "DOWN," and since they could soon see houses quite clearly, they knew they would be home before long.

The sailor remarked to Raggedy Ann, "It will be very good to be home again with my loving wife and loving children. I have not seen them for many weeks while I was sailing on the tugboat."

Just then the Captain cried, "Here we are, landing on the earth again!" And they could all feel the little boat gently bump as they came down and stopped.

The sailor looked about him and said, "Why, here we are only a few miles away from my little house. I shall be home in just a little time. Won't you come with me and visit awhile?"

Raggedy Andy answered, "Thank you very much, Mr. Sailor, but I think we must go on. Perhaps another time we will visit you!"

"Then thank you very much for rescuing me," said the litle sailor before he hastened off to his home and family.

"Mister Captain," Raggedy Ann said, "don't you

Gruelle

think it would be fun if we sailed the magical boat just above the ground down the path through the deep, deep woods. We are sure to have more adventures that way than if we sail the boat on the sea."

"Yes, I imagine it would be lots more fun," the Captain agreed. "For if we sail on the sea, another waterspout may come along and carry us way up in the air again. And that was really not fun at all! And we cannot be captured by Pirates in the woods either!"

"Still," Raggedy Andy said, "it is a lot of fun being captured by Pirates if the Pirates are only pretend Pirates!"

"Oh, yes," the Captain agreed, "just pretend Pirates are lots of fun, but if we should sail on the sea and really and truly be captured by real Pirates, then they might take our little magical boat away from us! And you know, Raggedys, if some selfish person should discover that this is a magical boat with a magical cupboard always filled with nice things to eat and a very fine magical soda fountain, they would be apt to take our boat away from us!"

"Ha!" Raggedy Andy cried. "I'd like to see any-one try to do that!"

"Aha! You would, would you?" a very gruff voice cried. "Just tell me what you would do, Mister Rag-gedy Andy! Just tell me, will you?"

"My goodness!" cried Raggedy Ann. "It's a Hob-goblin!"

"You bet I am." The Hobgoblin laughed. "And I heard everything the Captain said! Just let me take a look at that magical cupboard and the magical ice-cream-soda fountain! Just let me see them and I'll soon tell you whether I shall capture the boat and take all of you prisoners!"

"We shall not show them to you when you speak so rudely," Raggedy Ann said.

"Aha! Who says so?" the Hobgoblin cried as he caught Raggedy Ann and quickly threw her over the side of the boat to the ground.

He could do this easily because Raggedy Ann was very light, being made of cloth and stuffed with cot-ton. And because she was made this way, she was not hurt but only surprised.

"And who else says so?" the Hobgloblin cried as he looked at Raggedy Andy and the Hobby Horse and the little fat captain.

"I do," cried Raggedy Andy, just as loud as the Hobgoblin had yelled at him.

"Then over you go," the Hobgoblin screamed, catching hold of the rag doll and throwing him over the side of the boat too. But Raggedy Andy did not even stop smiling, because his smile was painted on.

"Now over you go, too!" the Hobgoblin cried as he rushed at the little fat Captain. But the Captain was too heavy for the Hobgoblin and, instead, the Captain threw the Hobgoblin over the side of the boat. And he hit the ground so hard that he saw a great many stars of different colors.

"There, Mister Hobgoblin!" Raggedy Ann said. "You see now that you got just what you deserved. Anyone who tries to hurt others always succeeds in getting into trouble himself."

And the Raggedys left the Hobgoblin sitting on the ground, holding his head, while they climbed on board the little magical boat where the Captain and the Hobby Horse were waiting for them.

CHAPTER 6

WHEN THE RAGGEDYS had climbed back on board the boat, Raggedy Ann decided to prepare dinner. It was easy for Raggedy Ann to get dinner on the little boat because all she had to do was walk to the cupboard and wish for whatever she thought would be nice. Then, as soon as she opened the door, she found what she had wished for! This time there were lamb chops, hot dogs on buns, big red juicy tomatoes, and crisp green lettuce chunks. And, with the magical ice cream soda fountain too, she knew they would have a very fine dinner.

As the little magical boat sailed along, they all ate every bit of their dinner, especially the magical Hobby Horse, who was the first one done. Just as they were washing their hands and faces, the magical boat came to a stop. So the little fat Captain ran out on deck to see what had happened.

It took the Captain only one minute to see why the little boat had stopped, for they had come to such a sharp bend in the path that the switch had to be set differently. But as the Captain prepared to reset the switch, he saw something that made him stop. There, sitting on a log, crying as though their hearts would break, were two people, an old lady and an old man.

"My, my!" the kind little Captain said. "Why do you sit on that log and cry and cry? Crying will not make the trouble go away, whatever it is. And all you will have for your tears are very, very red noses! And red noses really do not look very nice."

"We cannot help it," the old lady cried, "and we know only too well that red noses do not look nice. For we have just left an old Witch who had a very, very red nose, and it was very, very long too!"

"Well then," said Raggedy Ann who had come out to see what all the noise was, "if you have just left the Witch, there is nothing more to cry about."

"Oh, yes, there is," the old man said. "The mean Witch came to our little house and took everything we had, and then she drove us away through the woods. That is why we sit here crying."

67

"Can't you find another house to live in?" asked the kind Captain. "There must be many other houses in the woods that would do as well."

"But you do not understand," the little old lady sobbed. "We had so many nice things in our little house, and it is wrong for anyone to come and take someone else's house and things."

"That is so, and it was truly very, very wrong for the Witch to do that," Raggedy Ann said as she put her arm around the little old lady's shoulder. "You show us where this mean Witch is and we shall make her give back all your things."

So the old lady and the old man climbed into the magic boat along with Raggedy Ann and the little fat Captain. When the little boat, with its switch reset, sailed up to the old couple's home, the Raggedys saw that it was a lovely little house. It was white, with yellow shutters and a little red chimney poking out of the roof. And growing all about it were sweet-smelling flowers of many different shapes and colors. As the little boat came to a stop near the front door, the door flew open and the Witch with the very long, red nose poked her head out.

"You needn't stop here," the Witch yelled. "I do not want any fish today."

"We are not selling fish," called Raggedy Ann.

"Of course you are," the Witch called back. "People sailing in boats always want to sell fish, and I do not want any."

"See here," Raggedy Ann called out; "you'd better come out so we may talk to you. We want you to know how naughty you have been in taking this pretty little house away from Mr. and Mrs. Granny. Just come on out!"

'You can't make me come out." The Witch laughed. "The Grannys are too old to enjoy these things and this nice little house; that's why I took them for myself."

Raggedy Ann said as loud as she could, "Don't you know that it is always wrong to take things that do not belong to you?"

But the Witch just laughed again.

"I guess she won't come out," the little Captain whispered to Raggedy Ann. "You keep her at the window and I will run around to the back door and slip in quietly and then push her right out the window."

So while Raggedy Ann talked to the long-nosed Witch, the Captain tiptoed around to the back door of the little house.

After a few minutes, the Witch laughed and said, "Well, I see that I have also captured the little fat Captain. He thought that he could fool me, but I have magic on the back door and he is my prisoner now. If you do not wish to be captured too, you had better get away." And, with a *bang* the window slammed shut.

"Oh dear!" Raggedy Ann cried. "Now what shall we do? We can't sail away in the magic boat and leave the Captain a prisoner!"

Raggedy Ann, Raggedy Andy, the Hobby Horse and Mr. and Mrs. Granny tried to think very hard about how they could rescue the Captain. Finally the Hobby Horse had an idea.

"I think we shall have to wait until the Witch goes to bed," the Hobby Horse said. "Then I can climb into a back window, because I am taller than any of you, and I can get the Captain out."

The others agreed that this was a fine idea. Then Raggedy Ann suggested that they sail the boat away from the front door of the house and down the path into the deep, deep woods. "That will make the Witch think we are leaving the Captain and throw her off the track. Then, when evening comes, we can slip back and rescue the Captain and take the Witch prisoner."

So, finding a lemonade spring close by, the Raggedys and the Hobby Horse and Mr. and Mrs. Granny brought sandwiches and cookies from the magic cupboard and had a nice picnic. But it would have been much nicer if the little Captain had been with them.

Then, when the sun went down and the moon came out, the little group slipped back to Mr. and Mrs. Granny's house very quietly and listened at the door to find out if the Witch had gone to bed yet.

"I can hear her bustling about," Raggedy Andy whispered. "What in the world can she be doing so late?"

In a few moments they found out. Hearing a whistle that sounded as though it came from the housetop, they looked up and there they saw another Witch with a long red nose sitting on the chimney.

When the Witch on the chimney had whistled twice, the Witch inside the house stuck her head out the window and asked, "Witch Wiggle , do you see the Raggedys anywhere?"

And Witch Wiggle replied, "I can't see them anywhere, Witch Grundy."

So Witch Grundy banged the window shut and in a few minutes came up out of the chimney. Then she got behind Witch Wiggle on her flying broom and the two Witches sailed up into the air and away over the great forest.

"Now we can hurry and rescue the little Captain," Raggedy Ann said. "The Witch has forgotten to lock the window, so we can open it easily and climb in."

Turning to the Hobby Horse, Raggedy Ann said, "I think it will be better if you stay here to protect Mr. and Mrs. Granny, and Raggedy Ann and I shall get the little Captain out."

Mr. and Mrs. Granny were pleased to have the Hobby Horse protect them, and he was such a kindly animal that he was happy to do this.

Then Raggedy Andy climbed through the window and pulled Raggedy Ann in after him.

Then he told Mr. and Mrs. Granny, "You three had better go back to the boat and wait for us, for if Witch Grundy returns and finds you here, she may work some of her magic on you. We will be back at the boat very soon."

The Grannys got on the Hobby Horse's back and galloped away while Raggedy Ann and Raggedy Andy started looking for the Captain. They tapped on all the doors and closets, calling at each place, "Captain, are you there?" But at no place did they receive an answer. All was quiet except for the sound of their own voices calling.

"What in the world could the Witch have done with the Captain?" Raggedy Ann asked. "The Captain was too large to be hidden in any small place. Maybe he has escaped while we were waiting for the Witch to leave!"

But Raggedy Andy thought they had better search once more just to make sure they had not overlooked something that could tell them where the Captain was. And while they were searching, they discovered so many wonderful things that they could understand why Witch Grundy had wanted this little house.

In one corner they found a pretty old clock which chimed at each hour and then sang a soft, lovely song. It was a fine, magical clock. Then there was a magic frying pan that cooked many different things, a magic ice cream freezer, and a magic box which always kept filling itself with games, no matter how many might be taken out!

After hunting for a very long time, the Raggedys decided they had better think of something else, for they just could not find the little Captain. So they sat down in a pair of rocking chairs before the fire, to rest and think, but they had no sooner settled down than they both went sound asleep and they both dreamed the most wonderful dreams!

If the Grannys had only told the Raggedys about the magic chairs, this would not have happened. But the Raggedys did not know that the two chairs were magic and were made for old people so that they might sleep easily and have pleasant dreams.

When Witch Grundy returned at midnight along with her friend Witch Wiggle , she was surprised to find that she had captured the two Raggedys without even trying!

"Ha, ha, ha, ha, ha!" the two Witches laughed. "Now we have the Grannys' house and their magical things and we can easily get the Raggedys' magical boat to take trips in too!"

While the Raggedys were still sleeping and dreaming, the Witches carefully tied them and put them into a trunk in a corner of the room.

When the Raggedys awakened, they did not know what had happened or where they were. They could feel that they were tied up, of course, and knew that they were together at least. But it was very dark and still in the trunk, and they had no idea whether they were in a closet or the attic, or maybe a box.

But finally they could hear the sound of the Witches laughing while they danced for joy around the fire. The Witches, of course, were very happy that they had the magic house and would soon get the magic boat.

While the Raggedys talked about what they could do to get themselves free, Raggedy Andy was busy trying to get his hands and feet loose from the strings by wiggling and twisting, but it was no use.

After a few minutes they heard Witch Grundy say to her friend, "Let's go and look at Raggedy Ann's magic boat."

And the Raggedys could hear the Witches leave and shut the door behind them.

When the Witches reached the magic boat, they found Mr. and Mrs. Granny playing a game of dominoes with the Hobby Horse. They heard old Mrs. Granny say, "Oh dear, it is a very long time since Raggedy Ann and Raggedy Andy went to rescue the kind Captain, and they should have been back by now! Perhaps we had better go find them."

But the Hobby Horse answered, "Oh, no, Mrs. Granny, the Raggedys will return soon, I am sure. Do not worry, for Raggedy Ann can always think of something if they get into trouble."

As he finished saying this, he was much surprised to see the two Witches jump on board the magic boat. And Witch Grundy was laughing so hard that she could barely talk.

But after a minute she told them, "That is what you may think, Hobby Horse, but what would you say if you knew the Raggedys were tied up and stuffed in a trunk in the little house? For that is where they are, you know!"

Mr. and Mrs. Granny threw their arms about each other and exclaimed, "Oh dear, oh dear, now the poor Raggedys have been captured and it is all our fault!"

The Hobby Horse, however, comforted them saying, "Do not worry, I will kick these old Witches right off this boat. And then we shall go and find the Captain and the Raggedys."

Before the Hobby Horse could do anything, though, the Witches had grabbed him and tied his four legs together, so that now he could do nothing but squirm. And then they caught Mr. and Mrs. Granny and returned to the pretty little house with them, laughing all the way.

As they came into the little house, they made so much noise that Raggedy Ann and Raggedy Andy could hear them. And they knew that the Witches had brought the Grannys back with them, for they could hear Witch Grundy say, "So you thought the

Raggedys would help you and get us out of your house, did you?"

"Well," Witch Wiggle said, "we have put the Captain in a match box for we made him very small with our magic. And we have tied the Raggedys hands and feet and they are in that trunk, all doubled up in knots and they can never escape. Now we shall tie you up and put you down in the old dry well in the basement."

And that is just what the two mean Witches did. When they had finished, Witch Grundy said to Witch Wiggle , "It is nearly two o'clock in the morning. My, I am tired! Let's go to sleep now."

The Raggedys were not sleeping; they were wondering how long they would have to remain prisoners in the dark trunk.

"Isn't this a nice pickle?" Raggedy Ann whispered to Raggedy Andy. "The Captain has disappeared, so he cannot help us. And the Grannys are down the dry well in the basement, so they cannot help us."

Then Raggedy Andy hopefully said, "But there is the Hobby Horse; surely he will be able to do something—though I cannot think what he can do all by himself against those two mean Witches."

Of course, Raggedy Andy did not know that the Hobby Horse was tied up just as they were and could not help them either.

Now, down in the basement, poor old Mr. and Mrs. Granny were crying because they could not think what else to do.

Finally, when she was so tired that she could not even cry any longer, Mrs. Granny wiped her eyes and Mr. Granny's eyes with her apron and she said, "Well, we must not sit here and cry. That does no good. If we cannot think of a way to help the Raggedys and ourselves, let's at least sing some happy songs. Perhaps, after all, help will come from somewhere."

So the two old people started to sing all the cheery songs they knew, and very soon they began to feel better.

Just as they were in the middle of their favorite song, Mrs. Granny suddenly saw, at the top of the well, a sliver of light that had not been there before. She put the fingers of one hand to her lips and, with her other hand, pointed it out to Mr. Granny. Then

they were both very still as they waited to see who was there. And all at once a little head poked over the side of the well, and soon a little body followed as an odd little creature climbed down beside them. There, dressed all in brown, was a little man.

"It's Mr. and Mrs. Granny!" he exclaimed, as he held up a tiny lantern and looked at the old couple fondly.

The Grannys had never seen the man in brown before, but they were very glad that he was friendly and cheerful.

"What are you doing down here, all tied up, when you should be in your beds fast asleep?" he asked them.

Mrs. Granny told the friendly little man about Witch Grundy and how she had taken their house with all its lovely magic things. And then Mr. Granny told the little man about the Captain and the Raggedys trying to help them, and about Witch Wiggle helping Witch Grundy capture them after they had tied the Raggedys up. Although both the

Grannys talked quickly, and almost at the same time, the little man in brown soon understood what had happened to everyone.

The little man showed the Grannys a tiny door which had been in the wall of the old well all the time, and, after opening it, he guided them along a hallway which led, he said, to his own little home. The Grannys had never known about this little home under their own, but thought it was lucky for them that it was there.

"We'll just fool those two Witches," the little brown man said. "You know, I thought something was wrong upstairs when I heard your crying. And even though you finally started singing, Mrs. Granny, I had never heard Mr. Granny sing along with you before. That was why I thought I had better see what was the matter."

Opening the door to his home, he said, "Come into my house and sleep here for the rest of the night. Then in the morning we will try to rescue the Raggedys, and the little Captain and the Hobby Horse too!"

After he had shown them to their clean little beds, he left them and went to smoke his bedtime pipe, smiling as he puffed steadily.

CHAPTER 7

"Listen!" old Witch Grundy said to old Witch Wiggle as the two sat up in bed.

"What was it, Witch Grundy?" Witch Wiggle asked as she rubbed her eyes. "No one knows that we have the Raggedys tied up hand and foot and stuffed down in the old trunk in the corner of the room. And no one knows that we have the little Captain hidden in the match box. So close your eyes and go to sleep! In the morning we will board Raggedy Ann's little magic boat and sail away through the deep, deep woods."

"Yes, I know," Witch Grundy replied, "but something woke me. I thought I heard a sound like *scritch, scratch, scritch.* Maybe it was old Mr. and Mrs. Granny down in the dry well where we have them prisoners."

"Dear me! Do go to sleep!" Old Witch Wiggle growled. "How can the Grannys ever escape from the old dry well? Just tell me that!"

"Well, maybe I was mistaken," Witch Grundy growled in reply. "So I shall try to get back to sleep again." And the two old Witches were soon snoring loudly again.

But they had been asleep only a few minutes before Witch Wiggle sat up in bed, saying, "Listen! What was that?" as she poked Witch Grundy with her sharp elbow.

"How should I know, silly?" Witch Grundy retorted as she rubbed her eyes. "You can't expect me to stay awake and listen all night long for noises that aren't there. I didn't hear a single thing. Please do not awaken me again, or I will give you a hard thump."

Witch Wiggle listened a moment longer and heard nothing, so she lay down and was soon snoring as loud as Witch Grundy.

A few minutes later, something cracked Witch Wiggle right on top of the head, THUMP! Witch Wiggle hopped up and looked at Witch Grundy. "Why did you thump me, old Witch Grundy?" she cried as she pulled the other Witch's hair.

Witch Grundy gave Witch Wiggle's hair a hard yank in return. This made Witch Wiggle howl ever so loud that she gave Witch Grundy a thump with her fist. "I'll teach you to pull my hair and thump me while I sleep!" she yelled.

"And I'll teach you to let me sleep in peace!" Witch Grundy cried in return as she banged Witch Wiggle's head against the head of the bed. Then the two Witches pulled each other's hair and thumped each other on the head until they were both so worn out they fell back on their pillows again!

But they had hardly closed their eyes when something cracked both of them on their heads again. With a wild scream and howl the two jumped from the bed and raced to the door, for they knew well enough that neither of them had struck the other such a hard blow.

"There's something in this house!" Witch Wiggle howled, "and I shan't stay and be banged upon the head any more!"

And out the door she ran, followed by Witch Grundy. The two Witches ran far and spent the rest of the night sitting on a log, shivering and wondering what had driven them out of the little house.

In the old trunk, Raggedy Andy and Raggedy Ann had heard the Witches howling and Raggedy Ann whispered, "I believe someone has come into the house and frightened the Witches away."

And at that moment the lid of the trunk was lifted and a little brown man untied the Raggedys and took them out of the trunk. After he had explained who

he was, he went to the cupboard and got them some cream puffs.

Raggedy Ann and Raggedy Andy were ever so glad to be rescued from the trunk where the two Witches had tied them and placed them. And they thanked the little brown man very warmly.

"Oh, do not thank me, Raggedy Ann and Raggedy Andy! I am only too glad to help anyone who is in trouble. And as soon as I found out that old Witch Wiggle and old Witch Grundy had hidden you in the trunk, I waited until I knew they were asleep. Then I came into their bedroom and cracked hard thumps right on top of their heads."

"We could hear them howling even though we were stuffed in the old trunk." Raggedy Andy laughed. "You must have thumped them very, very hard."

"Oh, not so very hard," the little brown man replied, "for I do not like to hurt anyone, even mean old Witches. But I did give them quite a thump, because they were sound asleep, it surprised them so that they thought it very much worse than it really was."

"But tell us, little Brown man, please, how did you know that the two Witches had stuffed us in the trunk in the corner of the room?" asked Raggedy Ann.

"Oh," the little brown man said, "I live 'way down under the ground and a little door leads from my house to a hallway and that leads to an old dry well in the basement of this house. Very often I have sat in the old dry well to listen to kind Mrs. Granny singing as she went about her work up here. Last night I found the two nice Grannys in the old dry well and took them to my home. They told me all about the Witches taking the Captain prisoner and how the Witches caught you. They are fast asleep now in my two little white beds, so, while they slept, I came to rescue you."

"The two mean Witches with their magic charms made the nice little Captain so small they could stuff him into a match box," Raggedy Ann told the little brown man. "We had better find the match box and get the Captain out."

So Raggedy Ann, the little brown man and Raggedy Andy opened all the kitchen cupboards until they found the match box, and tucked inside was the little Captain.

"I can make him his right size," the little brown man said as he took a horseshoe nail from his pocket. "This is a very magic charm." And he rubbed the horseshoe nail and wished for the Captain to be his correct size and there the little Captain stood!

"My goodness!" The Captain laughed as he stretched himself all over. "I thought I would never be rescued from that match box. It wasn't a bit of fun being so small and being stuck in there!"

He started to shake hands with the little man but then he gave him a big hug and exclaimed, "Why, Bertie! Wherever have you been all these months?" And to the Raggedys he explained happily, "This is my brother Bertie and I thought he was lost!"

And Bertie, the little brown man, said, "I have been living down under the ground, right beneath this house. When you ran away from home to become a sailor, Mother and Daddy worried so much that I started out to find you. But, search as I might, I could not discover where you were. Rather than return home without you, I have been living in this little house under the ground."

"Then, as soon as we rescue the two nice Grannys and drive Witch Grundy and Witch Wiggle away for good, you two must return to your parents," Raggedy Ann said. And since this was just what the two brothers wanted to do, they all went down to Bertie's underground house to find Mr. and Mrs. Granny.

When they reached the brown man's little underground house, they went straight to the bedroom, where they found the two little Grannys sound asleep in the two little white beds.

"What do you think?" Bertie asked the Grannys when they sat up and rubbed their eyes. "I rescued Raggedy Ann and Raggedy Andy from the old trunk where Witch Wiggle and Witch Grundy had put them. And then we found the little Captain in the match box where they had put him. After I had made him large again with my magic horseshoe nail, I found out that he was my missing brother. So now, as soon as we have driven the two Witches away and are certain that they will not return and bother you, my brother Bertie and I shall go home to see our parents."

"That will be very nice," Mrs. Granny said, "for I am sure your mother and daddy have missed you both very, very much if you have been away so long!"

"I am sure of that," Raggedy Ann said.

Turning to the Grannys, Raggedy Andy asked, "By the way, can you tell me where our Hobby Horse is?"

And Mrs. Granny answered, "My goodness! In all the excitement we forgot the poor Hobby Horse tied up on the magic boat." And they told the Raggedys what had happened.

"After we catch the two Witches and punish them," the little brown man said, "we will have to rescue the Hobby Horse. Then we can hurry right home to our parents."

This seemed like a very good plan, so the Grannys

went with the Raggedys and the little brown man and the little Captain to hunt for the two witches.

"I'll take a nice long stick and give them many hard thumps!" the little Captain said. "That will make them go hopping away through the woods and maybe they will never return."

When our friends reached the old log where the two Witches had sat and shivered after the little brown man had driven them from the Grannys' house, they saw the footprints of the two mean creatures.

"They have gone toward the nice little white magic boat," Raggedy Andy said.

"Then we must hurry!" Raggedy Ann replied, "for if they get there, they may sail away with the poor Hobby Horse."

So everyone ran as fast as they could, and as they turned a bend in the path, they saw the two Witches racing for the magic boat.

"Ha, ha, ha!" Witch Grundy laughed as she turned and saw who was following. "We shall sail away in your boat before you can even get near us."

And the two mean creatures sprang onto the deck of the magic boat and started through the door of the cabin to turn the magic switch.

"Oh dear!" the little Captain cried. "We shall never be in time to catch them."

And this did seem true, for although he was ahead of the others, he was still quite far from the little boat. But just when it seemed that the two Witches would surely sail the little magic white boat away, the cabin door flew open and Witch Grundy and Witch Wiggle came tumbling out and fell, head over heels in the grass. And, as you would expect, they were screaming and howling for all they were worth. And then the Raggedys gave a cry of delight, for coming right after the Witches was the figure of their dear friend, Raggedy Ann's magic Hobby Horse.

The Hobby Horse, in a loud voice, was saying to the Witches, "After this you will know better than to come into this cabin and try to take this magic boat."

Witch Grundy and Witch Wiggle were so frightened that they ran screaming through the woods.

Raggedy Ann ran toward the wooden Hobby Horse and threw her arms about him and gave him a hug. She exclaimed, "We were on our way to untie you when we found that the Witches were ahead of us! How did you ever get yourself loose?"

The Hobby Horse told them: "After the Witches had left me tied tight, I looked all about me to see if there was some way I could untie the knots. But there was not a soul around, and at first I could see nothing that could help. Then I noticed a small nail sticking out of the wall, near the magic switch. Perhaps that is where the Captain used to hang his hat. Anyway, I was able to lift my front legs up by lying on my back, and I slowly worked the rope back and forth over the nail until it wore through and my front legs were free. This took a long time, I can tell you, and I was so tired I had to rest before I could get my two other legs loose."

Raggedy Andy broke in: "We are very glad that you got yourself untied and that you stayed here and waited for us. Otherwise, the two Witches might easily have captured the magic boat and sailed off with it before we could catch up with them."

In his woodeny voice, the Hobby Horse asked where they had been and what had happened to them. Raggedy Ann and Raggedy Andy took turns explaining, and they introduced Bertie, the little brown man, when they came to his part in their adventure.

"I wondered where you were all that time," the magic Hobby Horse said. "But I knew that it was my job to stay here and guard the magic boat until you returned. I am glad that I was here to throw them overboard and I do not think they will come back."

Raggedy Ann thought out loud, "No, I do not think they will, but I wonder if they have returned to Mr. and Mrs. Granny's house? We had better sail the boat around there and find out, right away!"

So the little magic boat, with Raggedy Ann, Raggedy Andy, the Hobby Horse, and the little fat Captain and his brother Bertie and, of course, Mr. and Mrs. Granny, sailed right up to the front door of the Granny house. And, sure enough, they could see the Witches through the little windows!

"Come out of there this minute!" Bertie, the little brown man, called.

"Indeed we shan't," Witch Grundy yelled back. "Do you think we want to come out and be kicked by that mean old wooden Hobby Horse again? We will not budge an inch!"

"What shall we do?" Raggedy Ann wondered aloud.

The Hobby Horse laughed. "Why, that's easy. If they won't come out, I shall go in."

So Bertie pulled a window open quickly and boosted the magical Hobby Horse inside. Then there was a noise that sounded as if giants were stamping about in the little house. A minute later, out came the Witches so quickly that they slid across the path and into the brier patch across the road! When they had picked themselves up, they ran through the woods, limping and crying and howling.

"Now," Raggedy Ann said, turning to the Grannys, "the house is yours again, and I am very sure the Witches will never come back."

CHAPTER 8

EVEN THOUGH they were very happy to have their pretty house back, Mr. and Mrs. Granny were sorry to see all their friends getting ready to leave them. They stood in the doorway and wiped the tears from their eyes with their pocket hankies. And, when Raggedy Ann and Raggedy Andy and the little brown man and the little Captain climbed into the magic boat and prepared to sail away, the two Grannys cried and cried. For, as you must know, when you have made good friends, it is very hard to see them go away and leave you.

"Dear me," the little Captain said when he saw the Grannys crying, "this will never, never do! We cannot leave them crying this way."

"Maybe they are afraid that Witch Grundy and Witch Wiggle will return and bother them again," Raggedy Andy said.

"No, it isn't that," Mr. Granny replied. "We like you so much that we do not want you to go away from us."

"Then I guess there is only one thing to do," Raggedy Ann said.

"And what would you suggest, Raggedy Ann?" the little Captain asked.

"We must take them with us. They would soon be friends with your mother and daddy, I am sure."

"Oh, we are certain of that, Raggedy Ann!" both Bertie the little brown man and his brother the Captain answered. "But what would the Grannys do, if they left their nice little house and returned to find that Witch Wiggle and Witch Grundy had captured it again? The Grannys would not have us here to help them and they would have no place to live."

"Maybe after they meet your nice parents and visit awhile, they could find a house close to yours and be able to see you every day."

"Maybe we could," both the Grundys replied, as they wiped their tears and stood there smiling.

"Then you can just go with us—" the little brown man laughed—"for we are sure Mother and Dad will be glad to have two nice people like you living near us."

"We shall bring all of our magic things," Mr. Granny said. "We have the singing clock, the moving-picture book and a lot of other nice magical things. And with these in the house, your nice mother will not have to do a bit of work!"

So the Raggedys and the others helped the Grannys carry all the magical things from their house and then load them onto the magic boat. Then the Grannys left a note tacked on the door which said

that anyone who wanted a home could come right in and live there.

"Now we are all happy." The little brown man laughed. "Let's sail the little magic boat toward home!"

And the little Captain laughed and saluted as he turned the magic switch and sent the little white magical boat sailing along through the deep, deep woods.

Sitting up on the deck watching the scenery were Raggedy Ann and Raggedy Andy and their friend the Hobby Horse. Near by were their other friends, the little fat Captain and his brother Bertie, chatting with Mr. and Mrs. Granny. And since the magical boat had a very wonderful magic cupboard which gave them anything they wished to eat, the Raggedys and all their friends sat and ate all kinds of goodies while they watched the scenery and listened to the pretty songs the magic clock sang.

At last, the little boat sailed along toward the house of the little Captain. And there, in the doorway, stood Bertie's and the Captain's parents.

When they saw their sons in the boat, they gave a happy cry and ran forward to hug and kiss Bertie and the little Captain.

"Mother," the little Captain said, "I have brought Mr. and Mrs. Granny home to visit with us. They have a magic clock that sings pretty songs, and a magic frying pan that makes doughnuts, and a lot of other magic things! And best of all, they are kind, sweet people!"

"Isn't that nice!" the Captain's daddy said as he welcomed Mr. and Mrs. Granny. "I know we shall all have a lot of fun together."

Everyone went into the house where they sat and ate and talked for hours and hours.

Then at last Raggedy Ann and Raggedy Andy said they must leave. Although their friends wanted them to stay on, Raggedy Ann answered, "No, we must run along, for there are so many nice adventures in the deep, deep woods and Raggedy Andy and I must find them."

So they kissed everyone and said good-by, promising that they would come back and visit some day.

Then Raggedy Ann and Raggedy Andy ran out through the flower garden, out the gate and down the path through the deep, deep woods filled with fairies and everything.

THE
GRUELLE IDEAL

*It is the Gruelle ideal
that books for children
should contain nothing to
cause fright, suggest fear, glo-
rify mischief, excuse malice
or condone cruelty. That
is why they are called*
"BOOKS GOOD FOR
CHILDREN."